KAYLA THE VEGAN

By Stewart Mitchell

This book was written in hopes of inspiring our youth, the future generations, to make ethical choices that impact our communities and planet in a positive way.

—Stewart Mitchell

Chapter One
A New Beginning

Kayla Thompson just moved to Atlanta from Brooklyn with her parents, Mr. and Mrs. Thompson. They enrolled her in the Maya Angelou grade school and she will begin sixth grade this year. Her father Mr. Thompson, packed her a lunch and walked her to school. There was a local fruit and vegetable market on the way, not too far from their destination. Kayla spotted it and asked her dad if it would be OK to stop in and pick up some fruit to take with her.

"Sure!" he replied. "What would you like to get?"

Kayla thought about it and said, "Just a couple of bananas and an apple."

"That sounds great!" said Mr. Thompson.

They entered the market and was greeted by Mr. Lee, the shop owner.

"Hello," Mr. Lee said with a smile. "Anything I can help you with today?"

"Yes, two bananas and an apple, please," Kayla answered.

As Mr. Lee put Kayla's fruit in a bag, Mr. Thompson handed him the money owed for their purchase. Kayla introduced herself to Mr. Lee.

"My name is Kayla. I'm new to Atlanta, and I'm about to start my first day in my new school."

"Oh, how wonderful," Mr. Lee responded. "I'm Mr. Lee. It's so nice to meet you. You're such a bright young girl. Good luck on your first day!"

Kayla and her dad took off. As they reached the front of the school, Mr. Thompson gave Kayla a big hug and kissed her on the cheek.

"Have a great day! I'll see you when you get home." he said. She hugged her dad back, smiled, and made her way into the building along with the other arriving students.

Kayla entered her classroom and was introduced to the students by her new teacher, Mrs. Johnson.

"Class!" she called out to get their attention. "This is Kayla Thompson. She's a new student who will be joining us here at Maya Angelou. She moved here all the way from Brooklyn, New York so be kind and treat her with the same respect that you would want others to show you!"

Kayla smiled and waved as she glanced around the room at her new classmates. They gave Kayla a warm greeting, some waving back and smiling too. Mrs. Johnson assigned her a seat in the row closest to the windows. Kayla sat down. She wondered if Atlanta would be anything like Brooklyn. She missed her old friends from her previous school and hoped to make some new ones in her new city. Once class started, Kayla gave Mrs. Johnson her full attention.

Mr. Thompson walks Kayla to school on her first day.

Chapter Two
Lunchtime

At lunchtime, all the children in Kayla's class made their way to the cafeteria. They stood around eager to eat and looking at the menu.

"They have the fish and cheese sandwich today!" said one classmate.

"I think I'm going to get the turkey with gravy," said another.

"What are you getting, Kayla?" asked another classmate. Her name was Brianna. She was the most popular girl in her grade. She took dance classes after school and attended soccer practice on the weekends. Kayla didn't know it yet, but eventually she would learn that Brianna was funny, brave, sweet and humble.

Kayla responded, "My father packed me a lunch. I also have some fruit that I bought from the market this morning."

"Fruit is boring!" a boy named Jayden exclaimed. "They have French fries and grilled cheese, I'm getting that today!"

"Don't pay him any mind." said Brianna. "That's Jayden. He goes out of his way to get attention and can be very annoying sometimes."

Kayla just smiled. Brianna took her lunch tray and walked with Kayla to sit with the rest of their classmates. Kayla opened her lunch bag and took out the contents, a spinach salad with cucumber and tomato slices with some olive oil, a small container of seasoned quinoa and a small portion of a lentil loaf her mom prepared the night before.

"What is that?" Jayden asked with a grimace. "It looks *boring*! Who likes salad? Why don't you go and get a fish sandwich? That would be a lot better than eating those boring leaves!"

Kayla responded, "No thank you, Jayden. I don't eat fish. I'm vegan."

Jayden looked puzzled. Then he said in a loud voice, "Vegan! What does *that* mean? You don't eat fish? Everybody loves the fish sandwiches here. What's wrong with you?"

The other children at the table laughed and giggled at Jayden's antics.

Kayla smiled and explained, "I don't eat fish, meat, or any animal products like eggs, cheese, or milk. There's so many good plant based foods that we can eat. I mean, animals want to live too, just like us, ya know?"

Her classmates looked at her in surprise. Kayla started to feel embarrassed once she saw the confused looks on their faces. The smile disappeared from her lips and she dropped her gaze down to her lap.

"Being a vegan sounds dumb!" declared Jayden. "Plus, fish sandwiches are awesome! grilled cheese is awesome! I love eggs and bacon in the morning, so I don't know what you're talking about!"

The children at the table thought Jayden's response was hilarious. Kayla started to feel out of place so she got up and moved to another table where she could sit by herself.

Brianna frowned at Jayden and said, "You don't always have to be so rude."

She stood up and went to join Kayla. Kayla was in tears because she felt so humiliated by Jayden's immature comments.

"He's just a class clown looking for attention." Brianna reassured her.

Kayla sadly looked at her new friend and said, "Now everyone is going to think I'm weird. I thought they would understand me."

Brianna felt bad for her new friend and tried to console her. She wanted to help Kayla but wasn't sure how.

Kayla started to feel like an outcast in her new
school.

Chapter Three
Making a New Friend

The next day at lunch, Kayla sat alone again in the cafeteria. She was too embarrassed from the day before to sit with the rest of the class. Jayden walked by with his lunch tray on his way to sit with the rest of the students.

"What are you eating today, weirdo?" he asked rudely. "More leaves?"

Kayla ignored his comments and just continued eating.

Brianna walked over and sat next to her.

"I noticed in class that you're pretty good with math." she said. "I have dance lessons after school but when I'm done, would you like to come over to my house and do homework together?"

"That sounds good to me." Kayla said with a nod and smile.

Later that day, Kayla's dad took her to Brianna's house. Mr. Thompson met Brianna's parents, Mr. and Mrs. Taylor. After speaking with them for a few minutes he told Kayla that he would be back to pick her up in a couple of hours. Brianna introduced Kayla to her mom and dad. They were delighted to meet her and made Kayla feel welcome in their home.

"We'll be in my room doing homework." Brianna informed her folks.

About thirty minutes into their studying, Mrs. Taylor appeared at Brianna's bedroom door and asked Kayla if she would like to stay for dinner. Brianna asked her mother what she prepared for the nights meal.

"Tonight, we're having chicken." Mrs. Taylor answered.

"Um, OK. Anything else?" Brianna asked. Her mother looked puzzled.

"Girl, why are you asking so many questions about dinner tonight?" Mrs. Taylor said.

Brianna explained, "Well, Kayla is vegan. She doesn't eat meat or dairy."

"Well, that's interesting," said Mrs. Taylor. "I did prepare some rice, kidney beans, and collard greens and I also made some raisin bread from scratch. Will that work for you, Kayla?" she asked.

"The rice, beans and greens sound great, thank you!" said Kayla.

At dinner, Brianna's parents asked the girls how their school day had gone. Brianna told them how good Kayla is at math. Kayla talked about adjusting to her new school. She also told Brianna's folks how nice their daughter has been to her, especially since the other kids have been pretty rude and unaccepting.

Brianna's father asked Kayla about her dietary choices.

"So Kayla, you don't eat meat? Your mom and dad support that choice?"

"My parents are vegan as well." she said. "They taught me to have respect for all living creatures. They also taught me that whole natural foods are the best foods for us."

"Well, where do you get your protein?" asked Mr. Taylor with a raised eyebrow. "It's natural for humans to eat other animals for protein. It's the cycle of life."

Kayla responded, "My parents make sure I get well-balanced meals. I get plenty of protein and calcium from the vegetables, grains and legumes my mother prepares for us."

Kayla captured Mr. Taylor's full attention.

She continued, "If we can get all of our nutrition without harming animals, why not? she asked. Kayla added enthusiastically. "Besides, animals just want to be loved, like us."

Brianna was impressed with her new friend and smiled at her father. "Dad, I think I'd like to try going vegan, too!" she said beaming.

Brianna's parents looked at each other and Mr. Taylor responded,

"I don't think that's a good idea, Brianna. You need your energy for dancing and soccer. I don't think you can get that from just eating plants. We'll talk about it later."

The next day, Kayla and Brianna met up and walked to school together.

"My dad gave me a few dollars to get a snack for later." Said Kayla. Would you like something? My treat." Kayla added.

"Sure! What are you getting?" asked Brianna.

"I know a great fruit and vegetable market on the way to school." Kayla said with a smile. "I usually get a few pieces of fruit from there."

They arrived at the market and were greeted by Mr. Lee.

"It's my new favorite customer!" he said with excitement. "Who is this young girl with you? A friend?"

"Hi, Mr. Lee. This is Brianna, my friend from school."

Brianna always walked past the produce stand on her way to school but she never paid it any attention until now.

"I'll get whatever you're getting, Kayla." she said. Kayla picked out some fresh grapes, two plums and a bag of almonds. She paid for her fruit and said goodbye to Mr. Lee.

When they got outside, Brianna had some questions for Kayla.

"If you don't eat or drink things that contain milk, I guess that means you don't eat ice cream or cake?" Brianna questioned. "Have you ever had ice cream, even *once*?" she asked.

Kayla laughed. "Sure I have!" Brianna looked bewildered so Kayla explained, "There are other things that you can use to make ice cream with besides dairy milk. My mom makes homemade ice cream using almond milk and bananas!"

Brianna was still a bit curious about what veganism is and asked,

"So can you explain again exactly why don't you drink milk?"

Kayla clarified, "When mother cows produce milk, it's supposed to be for their calves. So if we're drinking their milk, their babies are being robbed of their nutrition and the chance to grow up. It's not fair for us to take milk from them just because we can."

Brianna thought for a second. She realized that Kayla was making a lot of sense. "You know, I never thought of it that way. Maybe I should ask my parents to try almond milk!"

At lunchtime, the girls sat together and ate. They shared the fruit they bought earlier from the market.

Jayden walked by with a few other kids from class.

"Brianna, why don't you eat with us anymore?" he asked angrily. "Why are you always over here with the weird vegan girl?

Some classmates giggled at Jayden's comments.

Jayden arrogantly asked, "So now you don't like hamburgers anymore either, Brianna?"

The other kids bursted in laughter at Brianna and Kayla.

Brianna stood up, looked Jayden right in the eyes and said, "You know, if you'd put as much effort into your studies as you do into being an annoying bully, you'd be the best student in class instead of failing all the time!"

Jayden looked shocked and embarrassed as the other kids laughed at Brianna's remark.

Brianna continued, "Kayla is helping me with my math. She's cool, smart and even *you* could learn something from her, Jayden."

The group of students let out a collective, "Ooooh!" towards Jayden.

Obviously embarrassed, Jayden just shrugged his shoulders, walked away and waved his hand at her dismissively. The other classmates stood behind watching as he left.

Brianna was well respected among her classmates.

"You guys shouldn't laugh at someone just because they're vegan." Brianna said to them. "Kayla's very sweet and smart. All of you should get to know her."

Suddenly everyone felt ashamed of their unwelcoming behavior and they apologized to Kayla for their ridicule earlier.

Kayla and Brianna really enjoyed each other's company and were becoming close friends. Kayla went with Brianna to her soccer games and cheered her on. Brianna studied with Kayla after school improving greatly in math and was learning so much about veganism. She learned that everyday choices people make have an impact on the lives of other living creatures—for example, many lotions, soaps and cleaning products are tested on animals and some of the clothes people choose to wear like leather and fur are made from animals. Kayla also explained that animals in circuses are treated very badly, too.

"Wow, I never knew how much harm we cause other animals!" Brianna said sadly. "We make choices every day that cause so much suffering!"

Kayla responded, "Yeah, but we don't have to! We can still wear stylish clothes and use products that don't contribute to animal cruelty!"

Kayla gave Brianna a list of companies that don't test their products on animals and are also safe for the environment.

One day the girls were walking home from school and Kayla told Brianna her plans for the future.

"I want to be a lawyer and an activist one day, Brianna." she said.

"Animals can't speak for themselves, so I'm going to be that voice." she said with determination.

"Even though it hurt my feelings when the class laughed at me, it's nothing compared to what these poor animals go though."

Kayla and Brianna were starting to become the very best of friends!

Chapter Four
Questions and Answers

Kayla started making a few more friends each day. They were interested in hearing why she's vegan. Kayla and Brianna started to sit with the other students at lunch again. They all had questions for Kayla and she was happy to answer all of them.

"Doesn't it get boring just eating salad all the time?" asked a classmate named Messiah.

Kayla shook her head and answered, "I don't just eat salad. I can imagine that would be pretty boring."

Messiah looked baffled. "Well, what else does a vegan eat?"

"There are lots of different foods to eat!" she said enthusiastically. "I enjoy the same things everyone else does except my family doesn't use meat, milk, or eggs."

Deshawn, another classmate spoke up and asked, "Like what? Everything's made with milk. Cake, ice cream, cookies—everything I love!"

Kayla explained how these desserts can be made using milk and butter made out of different nuts, beans, and whole grains like almonds, soybeans and oats instead of milk from cows. She told them they can also enjoy burgers made out of beans, bacon made out of tempeh and all their favorite snacks made with vegan versions of butter.

Kayla also pointed out how much tastier and healthier these alternatives are.

Angel, another classmate asked, "But why go to all that trouble if there's already cake and cookies to eat?"

Kayla responded by explaining that life for animals on farms is short and miserable. She said that in order for the kids to enjoy their favorite foods, animals had to endure inhumane treatment. She told them about all the abuse and heartache the animals go through just so people can have their milk, eggs and meat.

"But isn't that the purpose of animals?" asked Messiah. "My parents said we need milk for good nutrition. Cows are here to give us milk, aren't they?"

Kayla shook her head in disagreement. "The nutrition we need is in plants, plus it's a lot healthier!" she explained.

"Do you think it's OK to hurt a dog or cat?", she asked somberly.

All of her classmates at the table shook their heads no.

Angel said, "I have a dog at home, and I would be really upset if anyone did anything to hurt him!"

Kayla replied, "Well, the same way your dog needs love is the same way all animals need love.

Cows shouldn't be hurting just so we can enjoy cheese, milkshakes, cake, or anything else made from dairy milk."

The children started to understand what Kayla was trying to explain.

"So if I can use almonds to make milk and soy to make butter," Kayla went on to explain, "I'd rather do that, than to have an animal suffer. Besides, we don't have to make these items ourselves—they're at the grocery store!"

The next day Kayla arrived at school with a big box of treats. She took it down to the cafeteria at lunchtime.

"What's in the box, Kayla?" asked Messiah. All the other children looked on inquisitively. Kayla opened the box and it was full of cookies, mini-cupcakes and doughnuts!

"My mom made these snacks for us to enjoy!" she beamed. "I told her that I've been speaking to my classmates about how delicious vegan snacks are and she thought it would be better to show you instead of trying to tell you."

The children's eyes grew wide looking at all the delicious-looking treats in the box. Kayla encouraged them to help themselves and share amongst each other. There were plenty of different snacks for everyone. Some children hesitated. They weren't sure if the snacks would taste like the dairy-based treats they were used to. The children who did help themselves encouraged the few that were still undecided. "

These are vegan? No way!" said Deshawn.

"These doughnuts are out of this world!" Angel said with a wide grin after taking a large bite.

"And you thought I was kidding, didn't you?" Kayla teased as she and Briana started laughing. All of the children were enjoying enjoying the pastries and happily chatting among themselves. Jayden sat at the end of the table alone. He was annoyed by how much everyone was enjoying the vegan pastries.

Kayla looked over at Jayden and said quietly, "Hey Jayden, there's plenty for everyone if you'd like to have some.", she offered. "I think the mini-cupcakes are the best. Would you like to try one?"

"Pffft! Cookies and cupcakes made out of grass and bird food?" he said sarcastically. "I don't think so!"

Messiah shook his head at Jayden and between bites of a doughnut said, "I don't think you know what you're missing, Jayden. This is far better than bird food!" The other children giggled and nodded in agreement as they thanked Kayla and continued enjoying the sweets.

Jayden rolled his eyes and scoffed, "Man, whatever. I'm not interested in weird vegan snacks!"
The students ignored him and finished the box of treats.

Kayla brought in vegan sweets for everyone to enjoy!

Chapter Five
A New Menu

Over the next couple of days Kayla, Brianna and a few more of her classmates started buying fruit from Mr. Lee's fruit and vegetable market.

"Oh my!" Mr. Lee exclaimed. "I see more and more of your friends every time you come here, Kayla!" She just flashed him a broad smile.

One day after school, Brianna approached Kayla with a cool suggestion,

"Kayla, I have a great idea! Why don't we ask Mrs. Johnson how we can go about adding vegan options to the school's lunch menu?!" she said with enthusiasm.

Kayla thought it was a great idea and agreed!

Brianna added, "OK, let's ask her tomorrow before class!"

The next day the girls headed off to school. Along the way they met with a few other classmates and stopped at Mr. Lee's market. They picked out a variety of fresh fruit, mixed nuts and dried cranberries to share and hurried off to make it in time for class.

Brianna told the other classmates what she and Kayla planned to do.

"We're going to ask Mrs. Johnson to help us get vegan options added to the lunch menu!" she said excitedly. All the other children agreed it was a great idea.

As they all sat in class waiting for the first period bell, Mrs. Johnson quietly took attendance. Brianna looked over at Kayla smiling. She could hardly contain herself.

"Mrs. Johnson!" Brianna called out as she raised her hand to get her teacher's attention. Mrs. Johnson raised her head and looked at Brianna.

"Is everything all right, Brianna?" Mrs. Johnson asked.

"Yes," Brianna assured her. "It's just that Kayla and I have something to ask you."

Mrs. Johnson took off her glasses and put down her pen. "That sounds urgent. What can I do for you girls?"

Kayla stood up and spoke.

"Actually, we were wondering if there's anybody you could talk to about the lunch menu at school."

Mrs. Johnson looked puzzled. "What's wrong with the lunch girls?" she asked.

Kayla explained, "We think it would be nice to have more vegan options besides the small serving of fruit and French fries that's available." she said with a big grin.

The other students in class murmured their support.

"Hmm, how interesting," Mrs. Johnson said. "where did you come up with that idea?"

"Well," Kayla began, "I'm vegan, and a lot of my new friends are taking an interest in going vegan too since I told them how much fun it is to eat delicious foods without harming innocent animals." she explained.

Mrs. Johnson nodded approvingly.

"That's a very good idea, Kayla!" Mrs. Johnson saw the excitement on the faces of her students. "If you feel that strongly about not hurting animals, I'm going to see what I can do!"

Kayla and her classmates were happy and excited! Mrs. Johnson told them that she would share their idea with the principal, Mr. Waters.

The next day, Mrs. Johnson told the children that Mr. Waters said that he would take their idea into consideration. They were excited to hear this, especially Kayla and Brianna. Jayden, stubborn as ever, didn't understand why all his friends and classmates were supporting Kayla and her idea.

"I don't see what's wrong with eating the same lunch we've been getting!" he said in an irritated tone.

"Nobody said you can't," responded Kayla. "But just think how cool it would be to have more cruelty-free options on the menu besides fruit and veggies!"

At three o'clock, the children headed home. Since most of them lived close by and took the same route, they walked together.

"Hey guys," Kayla said to her friends, "since y'all enjoyed the treats I brought in the other day, my mom said you're all welcome to come over and have some more!" The kids were eager and they all agreed to come by after asking their parents.

"It'll be great!" said Brianna. "We can do our homework together and have more vegan cookies!" Everyone laughed and agreed.

Kayla laughed and said, "As much as I enjoy my mom's snacks, I really love when she makes fruit bowls!"

Later that evening, Kayla's friends came by her house and met her parents. They all told Mrs. Thompson how much they enjoyed the treats she made a few days ago.

"I'm so glad you all liked them!" she said with delight. "I've made some more plus a few other things I think you might like."

The kids sat in Kayla's living room and ate brownies, cookies and cupcakes. There was also a fruit and vegetable platter with vegan dipping sauce. They loved it! They never had so much fun doing their homework before. They ate, laughed and genuinely enjoyed each other's company.

Chapter Six
Gaining Support

One day after school, Brianna's mom called Kayla's mom on the phone. She noticed a change in Brianna at home and wanted to share it with Mrs. Thompson.

"You know, since Brianna has been hanging out with your daughter, she's been eating a lot more fruit and she's even eating vegetables!" Mrs. Taylor said in amazement.

"Well, I hope that's OK," said Mrs. Thompson. "that sounds like a good problem to have." she added with a touch of humor.

"Yes, it is! Mrs. Taylor agreed.

"She's more focused in class and a lot sharper when doing her homework." Mrs. Taylor shared. "Also, her dance teacher told me that she has been much more energetic the last few weeks!" Mrs. Taylor continued. "But one thing does concern me. She has been refusing to eat meat a lot more frequently. She's talking about saving animals and stuff like that and it worries her father and I."

"Would you like to tell me why that concerns you?" asked Mrs. Thompson.

"We don't want Brianna missing out on any nutrients and getting sick." Mrs. Taylor stated. "She was raised on meat and now she just flat out refuses to eat it!" Mrs. Taylor seemed worried.

"I understand your concern but I wouldn't worry too much about it," said Mrs. Thompson. "You said it yourself—Brianna is more focused and energetic since eating more fruits and vegetables." she added. "If protein is your concern, you can give her more protein-rich foods like quinoa, beans, lentils and even dark green leafy vegetables— they're also rich in vitamins and minerals. If you like, I can give you some recipes."

Mrs. Taylor listened attentively.

Mrs. Thompson continued on, "Another good source of protein is plant-sourced meat substitutes at the supermarket."

Mrs. Taylor shared a little concern, "My husband and I were raised eating meat and we're in good health," she said. "Shouldn't that be good for Brianna, too?"

"Well, let me ask you this…" said Mrs. Thompson. "Sure, we can all sit down and enjoy a nice steak or chicken dinner, but do you think those animals wanted to die for us? No living being wants to suffer or die including animals. They feel pain just like you and me."

Mrs. Taylor shared, " I was taught growing up, those animals were put here for us to eat, but what you're saying makes sense."

Mrs. Thompson continued,

"I was raised on meat just like everyone else, but once I found out about the suffering involved in raising those animals, I chose not to support that misery."

"You know, you're making some good points," said Mrs. Taylor. "Brianna told me that she and Kayla even went as far as talking to the teacher and principal about including vegan options on the lunch menu."

"Yes, I'm aware of that," replied Mrs. Thompson. "I was thinking of starting a petition for the parents to sign in case they wanted to help support our girls."

"That's not a bad idea!" exclaimed Mrs. Taylor. "I think I'd like my name to be the first one on that petition!"

After conversing for a few more minutes, the two women wished each other well and said goodbye.

Kayla's idea was slowly picking up steam. The principal, Mr. Waters got word of the vegan menu from Mrs.Johnson and thought the idea was great, but he knew it wouldn't be easy to implement.

A few weeks later, Mrs. Thompson met with the parents and teachers at school. Some were a bit hesitant to the idea of a "vegan menu" so Mrs. Thompson explained to them the benefit of eating plant based foods and the potential dangers of eating meat. Even if all the parents didn't agree with the concept of "no meat" at the time, they all agreed that it would be great for their children to have fresh fruit, vegetables, whole grains, meatless versions of classic dishes as an option and dairy free substitutes. Mrs. Taylor was at the meeting and shared with the rest of the parents how much Brianna has benefited from eating more plant based, meatless meals in the last few weeks. The parents all signed the petition and Mrs. Johnson, who promised to help Kayla took it to the principal.

The following week, Mrs. Johnson spoke to Kayla after class. "Mr. Waters is really trying hard to have a vegan menu put in place for you, your friends and the entire school, Kayla!"

"That's great!" Kayla said with excitement. "Not only will it help us, it will also save a few animals' lives!"

Mrs. Johnson was impressed with Kayla's positive influence.

"You know, there's an essay contest coming up in a few weeks," she said. "Maybe you should write one about the benefits of going vegan.

If your essay wins, they'll print it in the school paper. How does that sound?"

Kayla liked the idea and agreed to write the essay. "Maybe more people will consider going vegan!" she said excitedly.

Kayla went home and started to work on her essay. She was ecstatic just imagining her essay in the school paper.
Later that night, she called Brianna and told her about it.

"Wow! How cool is that? If you win, you can show people how easy it is to go vegan!"

Chapter Seven
Spreading the Word

A few weeks went by, and the teachers that read the essays were moved and impressed by Kayla. She wrote about the importance of a well-balanced diet and the great health benefits of a vegan lifestyle, but more importantly, she explained how valuable animals' lives are and the importance of treating them with kindness and respect. The teachers agreed that out of all the essays submitted, Kayla's was the best.

The school paper printed her essay and the children in Kayla's class were excited about reading it.

Days later, more children were becoming interested in going vegan and choosing more nutritious, plant-based meals. The teachers and principal noticed how much the children's dietary habits changed since the article was printed. Kids were asking for more plant-based food in the cafeteria. They were requesting veggie tacos, veggie lasagna, and other meat and dairy-free foods!

By now, everyone knew who Kayla was because of the essay. At lunchtime, she had more friends to sit with and talk to. Everyone wanted to sit next to Kayla and talk about veganism and their love for animals! Jayden who was never very friendly towards Kayla, finally started warming up to her.

"I'm sorry for the way I treated you when you first came to our school, Kayla." he said. "Do you mind if I sit here next to you?"

"Not at all." Kayla responded and smiled. She even offered him some of her vegan cookies. They shared, smiled, laughed and chatted with the other children.

After school, Mr. Waters called Kayla into his office.

"Kayla, I must say that I'm impressed with the positive influence you've had on the students in your grade. I want you to know that I'm working very hard to turn your request for a vegan lunch menu into a reality."

Kayla smiled and nodded enthusiastically. "That would be great!" she said.

"I'll be honest with you," said Mr. Waters. "It's not going to be easy and it's going to take time but I promise you, it's going to happen!"

"I understand," Kayla said. "small steps. Thank you for trying so hard!" She left Mr. Waters' office with a big smile. She couldn't wait to get home to tell her parents the good news.

She left with Brianna and the rest of her friends that afternoon and on the way home they talked about the great news the principal shared with her.

She felt so good about making a positive change in people's lives.

When Kayla first started at her new school, the other children made fun of her dietary and ethical choices. Now her teachers, peers, and their parents were starting to see what a kind and loving person she was and a positive influence as well. That made Kayla feel proud. It made her parents feel proud of her too. Kayla's positive influence made the children, who now call her a friend proud as well. Kayla showed them that in addition to helping animals, going vegan can also help you find peace within yourself, among your friends and in your community.

Kayla is so happy that she helped to make a positive change in her community!

Stewart Mitchell is an author and human rights/
animal rights activist.
He is from Brooklyn, New York.

Instagram: @vigilante_vegan
Facebook: Stewart Mitchell

Original publication 2017
VOICE4CHANGE LLC